DATE DUE

JUL 8 2012	
AUG 2 2013	
JUN 2 8 2014	

In Jesse's Shoes

Appreciating Kids With
Special Needs

BEVERLY LEWIS

ILLUSTRATED BY *Laura Nikiel*

BETHANY
BACKYARD®
MINNEAPOLIS, MN

In Jesse's Shoes
Text copyright © 2007 by Beverly Lewis
Illustrations © 2007 by Laura Nikiel

Design by Jennifer Parker

Published by Bethany House Publishers
11400 Hampshire Avenue South
Bloomington, Minnesota 55438

Bethany House Publishers is a division of
Baker Publishing Group, Grand Rapids, Michigan.

Printed in China.

ISBN-13: 978-0-7642-0313-8
ISBN-10: 0-7642-0313-4

Library of Congress Cataloging-in-Publication data applied for.

"Before you criticize someone, walk a mile in his shoes."

—source unknown

To
Sandra, David, and Sarah
and
Lowell and Susan,
angels of tenderness and unfailing love
at the Stewart Home School.
B.L.

∾

To Pete and Patrick –
Thanks for your encouragement.
L.G.N.

Every day I walk my brother to his bus at the corner. It's not far, but it takes a long time because Jesse gets distracted by things like rain puddles, honeysuckle blossoms, and even ladybugs—which bugs *me* a lot.

Once when we walked to the bus stop, a bird flew overhead, and Jesse locked his thin knees and wouldn't budge. He stared up at the tree, his head flung back, eyes blinking. I knew it would be nearly impossible to get him moving again.

I guess I should be used to things like that.

Mom says God made Jesse special. Dad says that's true—Jesse's "wired differently." Our pastor says everything happens for a reason.

But *I* say—only to myself—"Why didn't I get a regular brother?" One like my friend Ashley's brother, Michael, who's eleven just like Jesse is. Except Michael doesn't act like a baby.

Jesse is who he is, I guess, whether I like it or not.

"C'mon now, you'll miss your bus." I tugged on his sleeve, but Jesse was in his own world, still gawking at the bird perched on a high branch.

"Sisser…not *listening*," he whispered back.

I shook my head. "You can talk to your silly ol' bird after school. Hurry—you'll be late!"

He frowned and shook his head. "No-o…no."

I sighed. *Just great.* If I didn't think of something quick, Jesse would miss his bus. I might miss mine, too.

Up ahead, I spotted Marcus Anderson wearing a bright red shirt. *Perfect!* I thought.

"Hey, Jesse, look," I said. "There's your friend."

Slowly, dreamily, Jesse lowered his head. Then he hunched forward and began trudging down the street. With his gaze on the red target, he chanted, "Marc-us…Marc-us…"

"He's going to race you to the corner," I said, urging him forward.

"Jesse run now," my brother said, wearing a goofy grin.

I tried to slow him down because he gets out of breath easily. But his eyes were fixed on Marcus, and there was no stopping him.

Several students from the neighborhood—ordinary, *regular* kids—were walking on the other side of the street. I knew which ones were already giggling, because this happened nearly every day. They were making fun of Jesse. Were they laughing at me, too?

At the corner, Jesse reached for my hand, but I pulled away. It was hard enough walking with your older brother like he was a four-year-old. I wouldn't be caught holding his hand, too!

Finally, I got him into the short yellow bus that would take him to school. He waved and grinned at me through the window, like I was the best sister on the planet.

"See ya later, alleee…gator!" he called, his nose smashed against the glass, eyes shining.

I watched the bus chortle away, not waving back. I could hardly wait to get to school with my friends.

The other kids crossed the street, still whispering and giggling. I noticed a girl with them I hadn't seen before. She was about my age and had a bushy brown ponytail.

"Is something…wrong with him?" she asked quietly.

"Not something, *everything*," another girl answered, and her friends laughed.

I tried to ignore them, but I felt my face burn red.

"Your brother's weird," said a tall boy about Jesse's size. He leaned his head back, staring at the sky the way Jesse did. "Duh…look at me," he teased.

The whole bunch of them hooted. Except the new girl. But I figured she would probably join in soon.

I wanted to run home, to get away from them. But I was just as bad, wasn't I? Sisters were supposed to stick up for their brothers—normal or not. But I was tired of being embarrassed by Jesse. At that moment, I wished Mom and Dad would send him away to a boarding school. One far from here.

All the rest of the day, I felt terrible for even thinking such a thing. I loved my brother—always had. It was just so hard sometimes. I couldn't help but wonder, why does he do the things he does?

Like, why *do* Jesse's words get mixed up? What he says is often hard to understand, like high-pitched mumble-jumble. But every now and then he surprises me and says exactly what he wants to say, loud and clear.

Jesse calls me Sister, even though when he says it, it sounds like "Sisser." He's never, ever said my real name. And when he writes *his* name, he makes a single letter. Just a big, jerky J.

At the beach, Jesse likes to kneel on the sand, twittering to himself like a helpless bird. He can stare at a single oyster shell for hours and hours.

And what can he possibly hear when he's stretched out on the sidewalk, his ear pressed against the pavement?

What smells does he sniff in the pages of books?

Why does he rock himself to sleep so hard at night, like he's crashing against a rough sea?

Why does he act so…well, *weird*?

One day after school, I was so frustrated I threw open our front door and burst out, "I just don't understand him!"

"Of course you don't, honey," Dad said gently. "You haven't walked in Jesse's shoes."

Just then my brother came in the door, but I looked away. Stomping up the stairs, I knew he was watching me.

I marched into my room and flopped down on my bed, feeling sorry for myself.

But something on the wall caught my eye. It was a picture frame I'd made at camp last summer. It read *God made me special,* with a photo of Jesse and me inside.

The same picture had been on my wall for months, but I'd never really looked at it. Why was I drawn to it now? Why was my heart so heavy?

"I'm sorry, God," I whispered. "You love Jesse just the way he is, and I should, too."

God made me special

The next morning Jesse had a doctor appointment, so Mom planned to drive him to school later. I thought I would be relieved not to walk with Jesse, but instead I felt lonely.

After school that day, I hurried to meet Jesse, waiting on the curb as he inched out of the bus.

He shuffled over to a wooden bench and sat down. "Sisser…you be me now." He leaned over and took off his tennis shoes. Then, he held them up in my face. "Dad say, 'Walk in Jesse's shoes.'"

"What?" I sure hoped he was kidding.

Jesse got down on all fours and began tugging at my shoes. He *wasn't* kidding.

"Okay, okay," I said, glad we were alone. I wasn't sure about this game he wanted to play, but I slipped my feet into his scuffed-up, too-big shoes anyway.

Flopping down the sidewalk in Jesse's shoes, I looked up at the feathery gray clouds, piled up like giant haystacks in the sky. Jesse stopped and pointed. "See…big tower?"

We locked our knees and looked—really looked—for a long time, watching Jesse's cloud-tower shift into a "fire engine." Then become "cotton candy."

After that, I knelt in the grass next to Jesse and breathed in the scent of a rosebush, my nose deep in its blossom. *His* idea.

Jesse asked, "Does Sisser *feel* it?"

"Feel what?" I had no idea what he meant. *How can you feel something that's supposed to be smelled?*

"Do what Jesse does." He patted himself on the chest. Then he got down and put his ear against the grass, listening to the teeming insects. "God make everything buzzy," he said.

I watched black ants scramble out of their tiny hills and smelled a caterpillar's mildewy coat. Imitating Jesse, I petted the grass like it was a green, hairy dog, enjoying its smooth yet prickly texture.

I remembered what Dad had always said: *"Jesse's wired differently."* I was beginning to see—and hear and smell and feel—just what he meant.

Later, at the busy corner, Jesse again reached for my hand. This time, I put my hand in his and held on.

"Jesse's shoes…fit Sisser now?" He gazed down at my feet.

I smiled. My brother was way smarter than anybody knew. "They're too *big*," I said. "I'll need to grow into them."

*In lots of ways…*I realized.

When we were almost home, I spotted the troublemakers across the street, pointing and laughing as usual.

"Time for your snack," I told Jesse, doing my best to ignore the kids. "Mom's waiting."

Smiling and still barefoot, Jesse hurried into the house. I stood there on the porch, not going in. Jesse turned and waved at me like he was saying good-bye for a whole week or something.

"There's the weirdo's sister," a boy hollered.

As the kids crossed the street and walked toward our house, I prayed silently, *Help me say the right thing, God.*

At last, I managed to speak up. "Different isn't weird. Or bad," I said as they approached. "In lots of ways, Jesse's just like you."

"No way!" two kids shouted.

"Yes, he really *is*," I said. "He likes chicken fingers with lots of ketchup. He's crazy about chocolate milk shakes and orange Popsicles. He's scared of thunderstorms and cheers at ball games with Dad. All that kind of stuff. Like anyone."

"Except he acts like a little kid, but he's bigger and older than all of us," said one of the girls.

The new girl shrugged. "It is a little strange," she said quietly.

I stood up straighter. "Jesse can't help it. He was born the way he is." I stopped to gulp in a breath of air. "The doctors said Jesse would never talk. But you heard him…he talks all the time."

The kids' eyes grew wide.

"He wasn't ever supposed to walk, but he ran a race at the high school last summer."

Now some of the kids stepped back, like they'd just heard a fairy tale. Or a miracle.

The tall boy said softly, "Wow…maybe some of *us* could've been born like that."

The new girl looked at the others. "I think we should say we're sorry," she said sadly. "Being different isn't bad. It's just, well…different."

A few kids mumbled apologies. Then, without laughing or saying anything more, they turned and plodded back down the street. That's when I realized I was still wearing Jesse's shoes.

The next morning, the new girl came by our house to walk with my brother and me to his bus stop. We left extra early, so Jesse could do all the things he enjoys. I even let him hold my hand the whole way.

I figure God knew what He was doing when He picked me to be Jesse's sister. And the other way around.

Halfway to the bus stop, Jesse surprised me and said my name. Not Sisser. My real name, Allie. For the first time ever!

"Wow, Jesse," I said, grinning. "You're amazing."

He teetered toward me and gave me a loopy sort of hug. I tried not to cry and hugged him back. Hard.

Maybe it's a good idea to walk in someone else's shoes, because I've never forgotten that day. And I hope I never will.